WIN A NAUGHTY FAIRIES T-SHIRT!

Every time those Naughty Fairies
are hatching a plan they do their fairy code
where they come up with NF words...

Niggle Flaptart
Nicely Framed
Nimble Fingers

Can you help the Naughty Fairies
find two more words beginning with
N.................. and F...................?

Each month we will select the best entries to win a very
special Naughty Fairies T-shirt and they will go into the
draw to have their NF idea printed in the next lot of books!

Don't forget to include your name and address.
Send your entry to: Naughty Fairies NF Competition,
Hodder Children's Marketing, 338 Euston Road,
London NW1 3BH.
Australian readers should write to:
Hachette Children's Books, Level 17/207 Kent Street,
Sydney, NSW 2000

Collect all the Naughty Fairies books:

Naughty Fairies

Potion Commotion

Lucy Mayflower

Hodder
Children's
Books

A division of Hachette Children's Books

Special thanks to Lucy Courtenay

Created by Hodder Children's Books and Lucy Courtenay
Text and illustrations copyright © 2007 Hodder Children's Books
Illustrations created by Artful Doodlers

First published in Great Britain in 2007
by Hodder Children's Books

1

A Catalogue record for this book is available from the British Library

IISBN – 10: 0 340 94431 5
ISBN – 13: 978 0 340 94431 8

Printed in the UK by CPI Bookmarque, Croydon, CR0 4TD

The paper and board used in this paperback by Hodder Children's Books
are natural recyclable products made from wood grown in
sustainable forests. The manufacturing processes conform to the
environmental regulations of the country of origin.

Hodder Children's Books
A division of Hachette Children's Books
338 Euston Rd, London NW1 3BH

Contents

Ambrosia Academy

WOOD STUMP

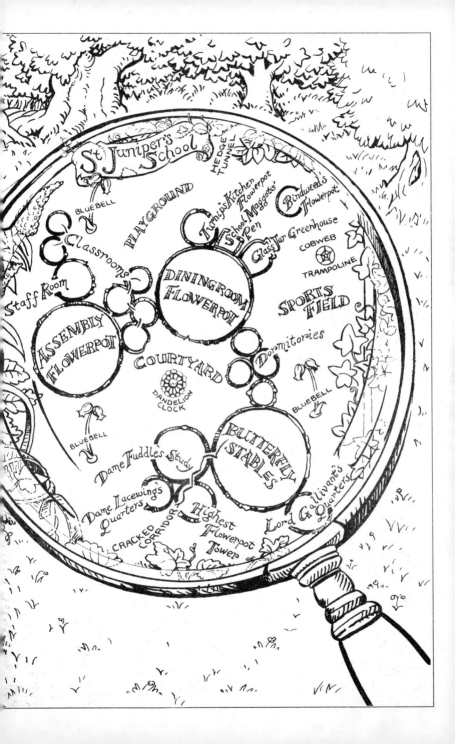

1

Pants!

Down at the bottom of the garden, something small and sparkly lay underneath the dandelion clock in the courtyard of St Juniper's School for Fairies. The courtyard itself was deserted. But from somewhere on top of one of the flowerpot towers, there was a giggle.

"Shh, Tiptoe!" hissed a grubby blonde fairy, wriggling to the edge of the flowerpot tower for a better view of the courtyard. "We don't want anyone to know we're up here, do we?"

"Sorry, Nettle," mumbled the little fairy who had giggled. "I can't help it. I keep thinking about the dew chew-hooh-hooh . . ."

The other four fairies on top of the flowerpot tower started giggling as well.

"Oh, for Nature's sake," said Nettle.

"Calm down, Nettle," said a spiky-haired fairy nearby. "Pranks like this are *supposed* to be funny."

"But nothing's happened yet, Ping," Nettle pointed out, fiddling with the tiny spiders that dangled from her ears. "And if we keep giggling, one of the teachers will come out and—"

The prettiest fairy put her hands on her hips and stared scornfully at Nettle. "Since when did any of us care about *teachers*?" she said.

"Brilliance is right," said a red-haired fairy in a black and yellow dress, who was stroking a very hairy bumblebee in her lap. "This is *my* flutterday – my first ever, since I only just learned to fly – so we have to do exactly what *I* want. And I wanted to do this prank from Ping's *Mischief Monthly* magazine. All right?"

Fairies had flutterdays every year to celebrate the first day that they flew. On a fairy's very first flutterday, there was a special breakfast, followed by a day out for the whole school. Today, the fairies of St Juniper's were taking a picnic down to the Pond. In the evening there would be a feast, with sugared buttercups and roast chestnuts, a hazelnut meringue and a flutterday cake to finish. Kelpie had asked for an enormous honeycake for her flutterday feast. Honeycakes were her bumblebee Flea's favourite food.

"We left Kelpie's flutterday breakfast early for this," Tiptoe pointed out to Nettle. "There were ants' egg omelettes and everything."

Down in the courtyard, the dew chew sparkled temptingly in the sun. A seed fell off the dandelion clock, and a nearby bluebell started ringing. Breakfast was over.

Fairies flooded out of the Dining
Flowerpot, chattering and stretching
their wings. As it was Kelpie's
flutterday, there was a festive feeling in
the air. The Naughty Fairies forgot their
squabble and leaned eagerly over the
edge of the tower to watch the fun.

A tall, thin fairy with a shock of
purple hair was the first to see the dew
chew. She glanced around to see if
anyone had dropped it. Then she knelt

4

down and reached for the little sweet.

"PANTS!!!" bellowed the dew chew.

The purple-haired fairy dropped the dew chew in terror and scrambled to her feet. From high up on the flowerpot tower, the Naughty Fairies screeched with laughter.

The dew chew rolled towards a group of gossiping fairies leaning against the wall of the Assembly Flowerpot. It came

to rest against one of the fairies'
starflower slippers.

"PANTS!!" the dew chew bellowed
once again.

The gossipers leapt out of their skins,
and took to the sky in a whirl of wings.

"I love this prank," said Kelpie,
wiping her eyes. "How long do the
effects last, Ping?"

Ping pulled a tightly folded orange
leaf out of her pocket and smoothed it
out. "The inactivated spell will last
eight dandelions," she read. "As soon as
the spell is activated, the effects will
last for twenty dandelion seeds, with
the voice getting quieter each time until
it can no longer be heard," she read.
She looked up at the others and gave a
wicked grin. "I've dabbed it somewhere
else too."

"Where?" breathed Kelpie in delight.

"Not telling," said Ping cheerfully.
"You'll have to wait and see."

"PANTS!" the dew chew shouted, as another fairy tried to pick it up.

The Naughty Fairies howled with laughter again.

"Ow," said Tiptoe, holding her sides. "Why does laughing hurt so much?"

"Does it always have to say 'pants'?" asked Nettle, fighting to catch her breath.

"Depends on the ingredients," said Ping, putting her leaf magazine away. "I used Plantain, Awlwort, Nodding Thistle and Saxifrage for this one. P, A, N, T, S – see?"

The bluebell in the courtyard rang again. Fairies streamed towards the Assembly Flowerpot from all directions.

"We'd better go down," said Brilliance. "Dame Fuddle will make her usual flutterday speech in the Assembly Flowerpot before we go to the Pond."

"Even Dame Fuddle would notice if the flutterday fairy wasn't there to hear her own speech," said Ping.

Dame Fuddle was the Head of St Juniper's. Large and enthusiastic, Dame Fuddle spoke in exclamation marks and never had a bad word to say about her pupils – even when her pupils were extremely naughty, which was most of the time.

"Wait!" hissed Nettle suddenly, as they prepared to jump off the flowerpot tower. "It's Dame Lacewing!"

A tall, fierce-looking fairy in a grey cobweb-silk gown was walking across the courtyard towards the Assembly Flowerpot. Dame Lacewing's pet rainbow-leaf beetle, Pipsqueak, scuttled at her feet.

"Has she seen us?" whispered Sesame anxiously.

"More importantly," said Ping, biting her lip, "has she seen the dew chew?"

Dame Lacewing hadn't seen the dew chew. But Pipsqueak had. As the

Deputy Head strode past the dandelion
clock, the greedy little beetle darted
towards the sweet.

"*Pants!*"

The dew chew's voice was quieter,
but still enough to make Pipsqueak
honk with fright and jump into the arms
of a very surprised Dame Lacewing.

"Come down here this instant,
Brilliance," said Dame Lacewing,
without even looking up. "And bring
your friends with you."

The Naughty Fairies flew sulkily
down to the courtyard. As usual, Tiptoe
tripped over her feet as she landed. She
flung out her hands to save herself, and
touched the dew chew.

"Pants," said the sweet
conversationally.

"That has nothing to do with you, I
suppose," said Dame Lacewing, patting
her nervous beetle.

The Naughty Fairies shook their

heads on the off-chance that Dame Lacewing might believe them.

"Detentions," said Dame Lacewing.

The Naughty Fairies all began talking at once.

"But Dame Lacewing . . ."

"It was just a little joke . . ."

"It's Kelpie's first flutterday today!" said Ping. "We're supposed to be going to the Pond in half a dandelion's time!"

"You should have thought of that before making potions you don't understand and scaring my beetle," said Dame Lacewing. "Report to Turnip in the school kitchen immediately. You can help him to pack up the flutterday picnic. I will tell Dame Fuddle that the flutterday fairy won't be there to hear her own flutterday speech. I'm sure she will understand."

And before the Naughty Fairies could protest, Dame Lacewing tucked her beetle under her arm and strode away.

"Pants," squeaked the dew chew.

"Oh, and pants to you too," said Kelpie irritably.

2

The Golden Violet

"Ye'll make the sandwiches," said
Turnip the kitchen pixie, as soon as
the Naughty Fairies trooped into his
kitchen.

A red-faced, red-haired pixie with a
bright red temper to match, Turnip was
the second scariest teacher at St
Juniper's after Dame Lacewing. He
often threw boiled pignuts at fairies
who didn't listen during cookery
classes. Brilliance, who had been hit by
a pignut *and* a beech nut during the
same cookery class, had told the others
that pignuts hurt a lot more.

Turnip handed the Naughty Fairies
some sharp splinter knives. "Ye'll find

the fillings over there," he grunted, before turning back to a large bowl of walnut and rosehip salad he was preparing.

The fairies stared in dismay at the piles of cornbread and sandwich fillings that towered towards the ceiling. Shredded daisy hearts, hard-boiled beetles' eggs, aphid cheese and minced chives, rose-hip pickle, sorrel spread and gooseberry slices.

"I can't believe I'm making sandwiches on my own flutterday," Kelpie growled. "How come Flea's outside enjoying the sunshine and I'm not?"

The Naughty Fairies watched Flea zoom joyfully past the kitchen window on his back.

"This is going to take all day," moaned Sesame.

Ping pushed up her sleeves and attacked the first piece of cornbread

with her splinter knife. "No *way* are we
missing Kelpie's very first flutterday,"
she said. "Get moving, you lazy dopes."

Grumbling, the Naughty Fairies set to
work. Turnip prowled up and down the
kitchen behind them, smacking his
hand with his wooden spoon and
making the fairies jump. Brilliance

expected a boiled pignut behind the ear
at any moment.

"Not bad," Turnip grunted half a
dandelion later, as the exhausted fairies
collapsed in a heap on the kitchen floor.
Piles of multicoloured sandwiches
spiralled up around them, teetering
dangerously on leaf plates. "Now ye've

to load up Caddy and the other
hoppers, and we're away."

Caddy was the school grasshopper.
He was large and solemn-looking and

could jump higher than St Juniper's highest flowerpot tower.

"Other hoppers?" said Kelpie. "I thought you only had Caddy."

Turnip scratched his beard. "Caddy had babies," he said.

"I thought Caddy was a boy," said Tiptoe with a frown.

"Ach," Turnip sighed. "So did I."

"Baby grasshoppers!" gasped Sesame. "How cute!"

"Cute enough," Turnip grunted. "If ye like that sort of thing."

He motioned outside the kitchen flowerpot to where Caddy was tethered. Standing beside the grasshopper were five youngsters. Although they were only a few days old, they were already almost as big as their mother.

"What are their names?" asked Nettle, as the Naughty Fairies clustered around the babies.

"Birdie, Bogie, Albie, Mashie and

Niblick," said Turnip. "Watch out for Niblick. He's a widdler."

The smallest grasshopper lifted up a leg and widdled on the grass, missing Ping's foot by a millisquirt.

"Urgh," Ping said.

"Aah," Sesame sighed.

The Naughty Fairies slung the baskets over the backs of the young grasshoppers and packed them tightly with the flutterday picnic food. The youngsters kicked and wriggled and sniffed at the sandwiches, while Caddy stood as still and patient as a stone.

At last, the grasshoppers were ready to go.

"Ye'd best join the others in the courtyard," said Turnip, taking a firm hold of six grass harnesses. "We'll see ye at the Pond."

The Naughty Fairies washed their hands thankfully and raced back through the kitchen and into the Dining

Flowerpot. Now Kelpie's flutterday could really begin.

"Hey!" Nettle grabbed Brilliance's arm as the fairies flew through the Dining Flowerpot. She pointed at a strange, glowing shape on the wall above the Dining Flowerpot's double doors. "What's that?"

The Naughty Fairies stopped and peered up at the shape.

"It looks like a flower," said Brilliance. "Don't you think?"

As the fairies looked, the flower shape glowed a little harder. It looked a bit like a violet, with two petals at the top and three at the bottom. On each petal, a golden letter swam slowly into view.

"F," Ping read, squinting hard as the letters took shape. "A."

"R," added Sesame.

"T," said Tiptoe.

"And S!" said Kelpie in delight. "That spells—"

"We know what it *spells*," Nettle interrupted. "But what does it *mean*?"

Beneath the golden violet, an image of crossed wands appeared. And then the whole thing faded away like a sunset.

"Weird," said Brilliance.

"Cool," said Kelpie.

"I've seen those crossed wands before," said Nettle with a frown. "But I can't remember where."

The fairies looked at each other.

"Do you think we should tell the teachers?" asked Sesame.

"Probably," said Ping.

They pushed open the double doors. A cheer went up as the other fairies caught sight of Kelpie.

"Kelpie dear!" Dame Fuddle came hurrying over. She clasped Kelpie's hands in her warm, soft palms. "Happy flutterday! Ah! Sweet memories of that first flight!"

Flea appeared with a red spider-silk ribbon tied jauntily around his neck and landed in Kelpie's arms. Dame Honey, the Fairy English teacher, leapt into the air on sparkling wings and landed on top of a flowerpot tower. She lifted her hands and began to conduct St Juniper's traditional flutterday song.

"Happy flutterday, happy flutterday, may your skies be blue," sang the fairies. "May the sunlight follow you-hoo the whole day through."

"Happy flutterday, happy flutterday, may your dreams come true," warbled Lord Gallivant the butterfly-riding teacher in a surprisingly deep and tuneful voice.

"May the moonlight follow you-hoo the whole night through!" finished the fairies.

There was another cheer. Grinning and high-fiving their friends in the sunlight, the Naughty Fairies forgot all

about the strange golden violet they
had seen on the Dining Flowerpot wall.

"This is going to be the best flutterday
ever," said Nettle.

"That's fine by me," Kelpie said.
"Just promise there won't be any
more singing."

3

Pond Life

The departure for the Pond was chaotic.
Fairies jostled and shouted, pinched
and wriggled, giggled and played tag
around the dented-looking dandelion
clock while the teachers checked and
rechecked their registers. Those fairies
who owned butterflies were racing
them between the crumbling flowerpot
towers, ducking low to avoid the strings
of petal pants and bluebell blouses
hanging out in the bright sunlight to
dry. The rest flew on a ragged collection
of school butterflies, or rode on large
creepy crawlies. Ping, Tiptoe, Brilliance
and Nettle were all riding Ping's
dragonfly Pong, and Sesame was on her

magificent Brimstone butterfly, Sulphur.
Kelpie was riding Flea.

"Hold hands!" Dame Fuddle
twittered, almost losing her large leaf
sunhat as a fairy on a Meadow Blue
butterfly swooped too low overhead.
"Keep in line!"

"Everyone ready?" asked Lord Gallivant, from high above on the back of his Red Admiral butterfly, Plankton. "Then follow me!"

He zoomed towards the Hedge.

"The Pond is the other way, Gracious," Dame Lacewing said. She kicked her Meadow Brown butterfly into action, holding Pipsqueak firmly under her arm.

"I like your sunglasses, Kelpie," said Tiptoe, as the Naughty Fairies flew in a straggly line after Dame Lacewing.

Kelpie took off her sunglasses and admired them as Flea furiously buzzed his wings beneath her. "I made them," she said. "In Fairy Science."

"I don't remember Dame Taffeta teaching that," said Sesame.

"She didn't," said Kelpie, putting her sunglasses back on.

At last, the whole school arrived at the Pond. Miraculously no one had got

lost on the way. The Naughty Fairies found a sunny patch of sand beside a smooth grey rock. Flea immediately fell asleep, and Sesame and Ping tethered Sulphur and Pong to a nearby twig. Brilliance dragged a shiny green leaf across the sand and spread it out beside the water's edge. She lay down with a sigh of contentment.

"This is all too good to be true," said Nettle, lying on her front on top of the grey rock.

Dame Lacewing clapped her hands. "Attention please," she said.

"Uh oh," said Sesame.

"SPARCLE regulations state that flutterdays cannot interfere with fairy schoolwork," Dame Lacewing continued. "Therefore there will be lessons as usual this morning."

Kelpie dropped Flea's grooming thistle. "*Lessons?*" she said. "On my *flutterday*?"

"What's SPARCLE?" asked Tiptoe.

"Don't you remember?" said Brilliance. "Dame Fuddle went to the conference last year. It stands for Senior Peering something."

"Peering at what?" Sesame asked.

"The Senior Peris' Annual Reunion Conference for Learning and Education," said Ping, coming back from brushing Pong.

"How did you remember that?" Sesame gasped.

"I nearly got thrown out of St Juniper's for putting a spell on Dame Fuddle at the last SPARCLE conference," said Ping. "I'm not likely to forget what it stands for, am I? They have meetings about teaching fairies the right things and do school inspections and stuff like that."

"But you're not *supposed* to have lessons on a beach," said Kelpie in a dogged voice.

"Sometimes I really hate being a fairy," said Tiptoe.

"At least we've got English with Dame Honey," said Nettle. "Pelly's got Maths with Dame Lacewing."

The Naughty Fairies cheered up. Dame Honey was their favourite teacher. They followed their classmates to one end of the beach, where Dame Honey was waiting. Pebble chairs had been laid out in a semi-circle. The fairies sat down expectantly.

"Apostrophes," said Dame Honey.

The fairies groaned.

"I'm brilliant at astroffapees," said Brilliance.

Dame Honey waved her wand. *"Rana!"* she called.

There was a spluttering sound in the Pond. The fairies squealed and lifted up their feet as dozens of wriggly black things launched out of the water and on to the beach.

"Those aren't apostrophes," said Nettle. "They're tadpoles."

"Today," said Dame Honey, "they are apostrophes."

She wrote something in the beach sand with her wand.

ITS

The fairies looked unimpressed.

"It's just ITS, Dame Honey," said Kelpie.

"Useful sentence," said Dame Honey.

She wrote ITS JUST ITS in the sand. Then she picked up a tadpole and tucked it neatly into place.

The sentence now said IT'S JUST ITS.

"*It's* with a tadpole means *it is*," Dame Honey said. "*Its* without a tadpole is like his or her. His wings, her friends – its wand. Got it?"

The tadpole hiccupped and fell asleep. The other tadpoles wriggled impatiently.

"Take one tadpole for each group," said Dame Honey, "and copy this sentence." She wrote ITS ITS TURN in the sand with a flourish. "Then try and put your tadpole in the right place."

Giggling, the fairies scooped up the wriggling tadpoles.

"Our tadpole is the sweetest," said Sesame, sitting down with a tadpole on her lap while the other Naughty Fairies wrote Dame Honey's sentence in the sand. "I'm going to call it Squiggle."

Squiggle burped.

"Ew," said Tiptoe. "Pond breath."

"Put Squiggle in our sentence, Sesame," ordered Brilliance.

Sesame stared at ITS ITS TURN. "Where?" she asked doubtfully.

Brilliance tutted. "Don't ask me," she said.

"I thought you were brilliant at apostrophes," said Ping.

The Naughty Fairies took turns

plopping Squiggle into the sentence. Brilliance was pleased with ITS ITS T'URN, until Kelpie pointed out that it didn't make sense. At last, they decided on IT'S ITS TURN.

"It . . . is . . . its . . . turn," said Nettle slowly. "That's like saying, it is his turn, or her turn – right?" She raised her eyebrows at the others.

"Time's up," said Dame Honey, clapping her hands. "What have you ended up with?"

"A frog," said a worried voice near the water's edge.

Her tadpole gave a *ribbet* and hopped back into the Pond.

While Dame Honey found another tadpole for the frog fairy, the Naughty Fairies double-checked their sentence.

I'TS ITS TURN

Kelpie tutted. "Squiggle moved," she said.

The little tadpole stared beadily at the

Naughty Fairies as it wriggled a bit
closer to the Pond.

'ITS ITS TURN

"Sesame, can't you make Squiggle
stay where we put him?" said Brilliance.
"He's ruining our sentence."

Sesame found a bit of pondweed for
Squiggle to eat and plonked him back
into place. Their sentence said IT'S ITS

TURN again. The tadpole munched happily on the slimy green frond, and stayed where he was.

"Excellent," said Dame Honey warmly as she passed the Naughty Fairies five dandelion seeds later. "Full marks."

The Naughty Fairies beamed.

"We're brilliant!" boasted Brilliance. "Let's sunbathe now."

She tossed her wand carelessly to one side. It landed on top of Nettle's.

Nettle stared at the crossed wands lying on the sand. "SPARCLE!" she gasped.

Tiptoe looked round. "Where?"

"I just remembered the golden violet and the crossed wands on the Dining Flowerpot wall!" said Nettle. "The crossed wands are the symbol of SPARCLE! I knew I'd seen them somewhere before. We forgot to tell the teachers that we'd seen the golden violet!"

"Do you really think it's important?"
Sesame asked.

"SPARCLE's always important," said
Ping grimly.

The Naughty Fairies scrambled to
their feet and ran up the beach in
search of Dame Fuddle. They tore past
a sunbathing Lord Gallivant in a
luminous pair of primrose bathing
trunks, past paddling fairies chasing
tadpoles, through an excitable game of
beach cricket and over a complicated

net of cobweb-silk skipping ropes. At last, they found Dame Fuddle snoozing on a flat golden pebble beneath the bulrushes.

"Dame Fuddle, Dame Fuddle!" chorused the Naughty Fairies.

"Hmph?" Dame Fuddle sat up. Her hair was squashed flat on one side of her head, making her look like a half-blown dandelion clock.

"What does SPARCLE's golden violet mean, Dame Fuddle?" asked Nettle.

Dame Fuddle looked more fuddled than usual. "Who sparkled?" she said.

"Not sparkle," said Ping. "S,P,A,R,C,L,E."

Dame Lacewing hurried over. "SPARCLE's golden violet?" she said sharply. "Has someone seen it? When? Where?"

The Naughty Fairies told Dame Lacewing about the glowing flower on the Dining Flowerpot wall.

Dame Lacewing went white. "Why didn't you tell someone straight away?" she demanded. "You saw it more than three dandelions ago. The golden violet is SPARCLE's four-dandelion warning. Don't you know what it means?"

"No," said Nettle. "That's why we're asking, Dame Lacewing."

"It means," said Dame Lacewing, "that the SPARCLE inspectors are coming to inspect St Juniper's – in less than one dandelion's time!"

4

The Inspectors

"SPARCLE?" Dame Fuddle squeaked in horror. "Coming to St Juniper's? Now? But Lavender—"

"We must leave as soon as possible,

Fenella," said Dame Lacewing. "I will find the other teachers at once."

She strode down the beach. The Naughty Fairies raced after her.

"There were letters on the petals of the golden violet, Dame Lacewing," panted Kelpie. "F, A, R, T, S."

The others giggled. Dame Lacewing shot them a look of pure ice.

"What does it mean?" asked Nettle.

"It is the SPARCLE inspection code,"

said Dame Lacewing. "F for Flying and Fitness. A for Appropriate Environment. R is Rigorous Intellectual Development and T is Tidy Wings and Wands." She glanced around the beach and tutted. "Where is Lord Gallivant? And Dame Taffeta? I must speak to them at once."

"What does the S stand for, Dame Lacewing?" asked Ping.

Dame Lacewing looked distracted. "The Special Something," she said. "It changes with every inspection. It could be Spelling, or Social Skills, or Sausages. SPARCLE keeps us guessing. Why oh *why* didn't you tell me that you'd seen the violet sooner?"

Dame Lacewing stopped. *"Gracious!"* she snapped at Lord Gallivant, who was sunbathing beside an enormous bulrush. "Change out of those ridiculous primrose trunks and come with me. We must get everyone back to school *immediately*."

Rounding up excitable fairies is harder than catching feathers in a high wind. No sooner had Dame Lacewing found one group of pupils than Dame Taffeta had lost another. Lunch was off. The fairies watched forlornly as Turnip loaded uneaten sandwiches, salads and berries back on to the grasshoppers with the help of Dame Honey. Lord Gallivant strode up and down the beach with his hands behind his back looking important, while Dame Lacewing and Dame Taffeta flew around trying to find missing fairies. Dame Fuddle wept and shook and cried: "Oh my poor wings!" more times than the Naughty Fairies had ever heard.

There was a gust of wind. A handful of dandelion seeds dropped off a nearby dandelion clock.

"Five seeds left!" cried Dame Taffeta, bumping into Lord Gallivant as she grabbed at a fairy doing some last-

minute paddling. "Only five seeds left before the SPARCLE inspectors arrive! Oh Nature!"

"It's only an inspection," said Kelpie grumpily, climbing on to Flea's back. "Why have the teachers got their wings in such a whizz about it?"

"It's really important that St Juniper's passes the inspection," said Nettle as Ping and Sesame untied Pong and Sulphur from their tethering twigs. "If the SPARCLE inspectors don't like what they see, they could close us down!"

"So?" Kelpie said. She stroked Flea furiously. "I hate school. This is my *flutterday*. We've had lessons and now we don't even get a picnic lunch."

"All is lost!" shrilled Dame Fuddle, as fairies milled around in chaos.

"Never fear, Fenella," said Lord Gallivant, putting his arm around Dame Fuddle. "We shall make it in time. When I won the Midsummer Champion

Butterfly Race, the race almost started without me."

The fairies groaned. The Midsummer Champion Butterfly Race was Lord Gallivant's favourite subject.

"What happened?" asked Dame Fuddle breathlessly.

No one had ever asked Lord Gallivant to expand on his Midsummer Champion Butterfly Race story before. He blushed crimson with delight and opened his mouth.

"He got the toilet door open just in time," offered someone from deep in the crowd.

"Everyone ready?" Dame Lacewing shouted over the roar of laughter. "Straight back to school now. As quickly as you can!"

Somehow, the whole of St Juniper's rose unsteadily into the air and more or less headed in the same direction.

"Two dandelion seeds to go!" puffed

Dame Fuddle as they zoomed through the Nettle Patch. "Oh my poor wings!"

Fairies, butterflies, dragonflies, centipedes and grasshoppers tumbled over each other in the rush to get back to St Juniper's in time. They could see the fluttering lines of laundry catching the breeze, the flaking flowerpots and the towering weeds. In a breathless whirl of sand and tadpoles, the fairies of St Juniper's crashlanded spectacularly in the middle of the courtyard – just as the dandelion clock dropped its very last seed.

There was a blue crackle in the air. Three grand-looking fairies in long white jasmine gowns seemed to slip through the crackle and appear on the steps of the Dining Flowerpot. They glanced around the tatty courtyard of St Juniper's with horror.

Dame Fuddle adjusted her leaf sunhat, which had fallen over her eyes.

"Lady Pollen!" she panted, trotting across the bumpy courtyard towards the visitors and almost tripping over a clump of moss. "How good to see you!"

The roundest fairy nodded her rose-pink curls.

"Lady Rowan!" Dame Fuddle continued valiantly, as the darkest and most elegant of the SPARCLE inspectors brushed away a fleck of mud from the sleeve of her gown. "And Lady Larchwood! How marvellous! Truly!"

Lady Larchwood's shining white wedge of hair looked as if it had been carved from a block of snow. "Delighted to be here, Dame Fuddle," she said, sounding extremely undelighted.

Turnip ran into the courtyard, clutching on to the harnesses of six excitable grasshoppers. Niblick wriggled out of his harness and jumped over to Lady Rowan. He did a friendly widdle at the inspector's feet.

"Well now!" said Dame Fuddle brightly, trying to ignore the puddle of grasshopper wee. "Lunch?"

Lunch passed off without any of the usual food fights or detentions. The fairies of St Juniper's were much too interested in the guests to play their usual lunchtime pranks.

"These sandwiches are a bit crusty," complained Kelpie, from the Naughty Fairies' usual table by the door.

Tiptoe took a bite out of an aphid cheese and chive sandwich. "I think they're nice," she said. "The trip to the Pond and back has improved them."

"I don't think the inspectors like them," said Nettle.

"Lady Rowan's had two gooseberry slice sandwiches," said Sesame. "But she's only eaten the gooseberry part."

"She's too busy for food," said Sesame. "She's talking to Lord Gallivant."

"I think she fancies him," said
Brilliance.

The Naughty Fairies stared up at the
top table. Lady Rowan was fiddling with
a long strand of dark hair and laughing
at something Lord Gallivant was saying.

"*Definitely*," said Ping. "Lord Gallivant never says anything funny."

"Lady Pollen's taken loads of sandwiches," said Ping, craning her neck for a better view. "But Legless keeps stealing them."

They watched Legless the school earthworm lifting his deep brown head from his usual position underneath the table and taking a hard-boiled beetles' egg sandwich from Lady Pollen's plate. Lady Pollen was looking rather ill.

"What about Lady Larchwood?" said Tiptoe.

"She just looks like she's got a bad smell under her nose," said Brilliance.

"Maybe Legless farted," said Sesame. "Hard-boiled beetles' eggs can have that effect."

At the end of lunch, Dame Lacewing rose from her chair. The room fell silent.

"Our guests will begin their SPARCLE inspection this afternoon," said Dame

60

Lacewing. "We will follow our usual timetable."

"Huh," said Kelpie crossly.

"They will stay with us overnight and give their verdict at midday tomorrow," Dame Lacewing continued. "In the meantime, I expect every single fairy to give Lady Larchwood, Lady Pollen and Lady Rowan their *full* cooperation."

"Why is Dame Lacewing looking at us?" said Ping.

"Search me," said Brilliance, pushing back her chair as fairies clattered and shoved and shouted their way out of the Dining Flowerpot. "What have we got this afternoon?"

"Fairy Sports," said Sesame.

"Ah," said Ping.

"What?" asked Brilliance.

"The pants potion," said Ping. "I dabbed the rest of it on the trampoline."

That afternoon, Lady Rowan sat down beside the cobweb trampoline. She took out a splinter pencil as the fairies lined up for the register.

"Lady Rowan's writing something down already," said Tiptoe.

"Has the lesson started?" said Sesame in surprise.

"It'll be something to do with the condition of the trampoline," said Brilliance. "SPARCLE checks stuff like that."

"Well," said Ping. "Let's hope Lady Rowan doesn't check the trampoline too closely. The pants potion is somewhere on the rim."

Dame Taffeta took Fairy Sports. She cleared her throat and glanced anxiously at Lady Rowan. "Today," she said in a loud voice, "we shall be attempting the Sycamore Twist on the trampoline. I shall now demonstrate."

"Dame Taffeta never demonstrates," said Brilliance.

"This must be for Lady Rowan's benefit," guessed Sesame.

"No wonder Dame Taffeta looks

nervous," Nettle shook her head.

Dame Taffeta scrambled on to the cobweb trampoline. The Naughty Fairies held their breath, but the trampoline stayed silent.

"Bounce," Dame Taffeta said, jumping gingerly. "And twist."

"Whoops," said Kelpie as Dame Taffeta landed flat on her face.

Several fairies cheered.

"Don't mind me, Dame Taffeta," said Lady Rowan, in a deep velvety voice that matched her long dark hair. "You just carry on."

Dame Taffeta's second Sycamore Twist was worse than her first.

"Lady Rowan's going to fail us," Tiptoe moaned.

"Bang goes F for Flying and Fitness," said Nettle.

"No one fails *me* unless I want them to," Brilliance said sharply. "We have to do something."

Dame Taffeta struggled off the trampoline. "Now," she panted. "Who's going to give it a try?"

The fairies around the trampoline stared at their feet.

"Anyone?" said Dame Taffeta, sounding desperate.

Lady Rowan's pencil hovered over her petal notebook.

Brilliance poked Nettle hard. Nettle was the sportiest of the Naughty Fairies.

"I'll have a go," Nettle said.

Dame Taffeta looked relieved. "Now remember, Nettle," she said. "Bounce and twist."

Nettle bounced and twisted perfectly, then flew off the trampoline with a double somersault and landed neatly on the grass.

"That's more like it," said Brilliance.

"Lady Rowan looks impressed," said Sesame with relief.

"We won't fail F for Flying and
Fitness now," said Ping confidently.

Nettle rested her hand on the side of
the trampoline to catch her breath.

"PANTS!!!" roared the
trampoline.

5

From Bad To Worse

The trampolining lesson had collapsed in chaos and Lady Rowan had written an awful lot in her petal notebook. Unsurprisingly, the Naughty Fairies were now standing in front of Dame Lacewing's desk.

Ping opened her eyes as wide as she could. "We didn't do it on purpose, Dame Lacewing," she said.

Dame Lacewing leaned her elbows on her desk. "I wonder why I don't believe you," she said.

"I wonder why you don't believe us too, Dame Lacewing," said Nettle.

Dame Lacewing took off her glasses and polished them hard on the sleeve of

her gown. "You do realise," she said,
"that these inspectors have the power to
close down St Juniper's?"

"They'll never do that," said
Brilliance.

"No other school would take us,"
added Kelpie under her breath.

"I wish I had your confidence," said
Dame Lacewing. "You are all on
detention with Dame Honey after
supper. More apostrophe work, I
understand."

"Will there be tadpoles?" asked
Sesame hopefully.

"I won't pretend to understand your
question, Sesame," said Dame
Lacewing. "Just try to stay out of
trouble until after the inspectors have
gone, will you? That way, we might still
have a school by tomorrow afternoon.
Dismissed."

The Naughty Fairies left Dame
Lacewing's office.

"Two detentions on my flutterday,"
Kelpie sighed. "That's got to be some
kind of record."

Even though lessons had ended for the
day, the inspectors were still on the
prowl around St Juniper's.

"We're going to fail A for Appropriate Environment for sure," said Tiptoe sadly, watching as Lady Pollen wandered across the courtyard, poking at the cracks in the flowerpots. "Our buildings are really tatty."

"I don't suppose we've done very well on R for Rigorous Intellectual Development either," said Brilliance. "Lady Larchwood looked furious when she came out of Dame Lacewing's Maths lesson."

"She always looks furious," sighed Nettle, twiddling her spider earrings.

"What's left?" asked Ping.

"T for Tidy Wings and Wands," said Kelpie morosely.

"And S for the Special Something," said Tiptoe. "Sausages, maybe."

"At least Lady Rowan's having a good time," said Sesame, as fairies slowly started assembling outside the Dining Flowerpot for supper.

The Naughty Fairies watched as Lord Gallivant took Lady Rowan's hand outside the Butterfly Stable doors and patted it. Lady Rowan was blushing.

"That still leaves Lady Pollen and Lady Larchwood," said Nettle.

"I don't suppose you've got a brilliant plan, have you Brilliance?" asked Tiptoe hopefully.

Brilliance tapped her teeth. "I'm working on it," she said.

Turnip flung open the Dining Flowerpot doors just as Lady Larchwood stepped out of Dame Fuddle's study.

"Wing and wand inspection before supper!" said Lady Larchwood, holding up her hand. "Stand in line, please."

Sesame looked aghast. "My wand's dented!" she whispered to the others. "Lady Larchwood will kill me!"

"At least you've still got one," said Kelpie. "I lost mine."

"How are my wings?" Nettle asked anxiously, peering over her shoulder.

Fairies shuffled slowly into the Dining Flowerpot, past the eagle eye of Lady Larchwood. Nothing escaped the inspector's attention. Dirty wands were held up to the light. Wings were spread and fairies were instructed to flap them twice and cough at the same time. Lady Larchwood's face grew steadily more thunderous. "Fail," she said, as each fairy passed. "Fail, fail, fail."

"I don't think the inspection is going very well," said Ping.

"Lady Pollen's cheered up," said Nettle. "Look."

Lady Pollen was standing in the middle of the Dining Flowerpot with her eyes closed. She was sniffing the air in ecstasy.

"Hazelnut meringue," said Tiptoe.

Turnip had surpassed himself. The counters were piled high with clover buns, forget-me-not pasties, roasted chestnuts in sage sauce and a magnificent hazelnut meringue. A vast honeycake took pride of place in the middle of the staff table.

"Stop drooling, Flea," said Kelpie irritably. "The inspectors are getting my flutterday feast. It's not *fair*."

*

"So," said Sesame, as at last the Naughty Fairies finished their apostrophe detention and trailed wearily across the courtyard towards their dormitory. "What do you think the inspectors will decide tomorrow?"

"Don't care," said Kelpie, yawning.

"Of course you care," said Brilliance. "Stop pretending that you don't, Kelpie. Whether you like St Juniper's or not, it's our school. Would you rather go to Ambrosia Academy?"

"Yeuch," said the others.

"Ambrosia Academy is full of fairies who wouldn't know a prank if it bit them on the nose," said Ping.

"*And* they wear pink," added Nettle as they entered their dormitory. "*And* spider earrings aren't allowed." She unhooked the little spiders that hung from her ears and put them on her acorn bedside table.

"*And* they'd never let bumblebees

sleep on their beds," said Sesame.

"OK," Kelpie mumbled, pushing a sleepy Flea off her pillow. "I don't want to go there."

"It's time we came up with a brilliant plan," said Tiptoe.

The fairies looked at Brilliance.

"I think," said Brilliance, sitting down on the bed, "that Lady Larchwood is the problem."

Tiptoe nodded. "Lady Pollen loved the feast tonight," she said. "She'll be in a good mood tomorrow when they make their decision."

"And Lady Rowan's so busy making eyes at Lord Gallivant that she wouldn't notice if St Juniper's fell down around her ears," added Nettle.

"It's a shame a hedgehog can't pop up and eat Lady Larchwood," said Kelpie dreamily.

"Fail," intoned Ping in a Lady Larchwood voice. "Fail, fail, fail."

"I can't imagine Lady Larchwood
saying 'pass'," said Nettle. "Can you?"

Brilliance jumped up. "Naughty
Fairies!" she said in excitement, and
put out her fist.

This was the Naughty Fairies' code.

The others clustered around Brilliance.

"Never flimsy!"

"Nobbly flump!"

They piled their fists on top of each other.

"Nifty fingers."

"Gnome fleece!"

"Gnome starts with a 'g', Sesame," Nettle pointed out.

"But 'no' starts with a 'n'," said Sesame crossly. "Why doesn't gnome?"

"Ask the dictionary fairy," said Kelpie.

"There's a *dictionary* fairy?" asked Tiptoe shocked.

"Joke," said Kelpie, rolling her eyes. "Nodding fox."

"Fly, fly . . ." said Brilliance.

". . . to the SKY!" finished the others, and flung their hands in the air.

"Where's your copy of *Mischief Monthly*, Ping?" said Brilliance. "We've got a potion to make!"

*

81

The moon hung high in the sky as the Naughty Fairies crept out of the dormitory, through the Sports Field and out to the glass-jar greenhouse. The moonlight was so bright that they could see their shadows on the ground.

"Right," said Brilliance, pushing the greenhouse door open. "Ingredients."

"I still don't understand," said Tiptoe, as the fairies slipped through the door. "Why do we want Lady Larchwood to say 'pants'?"

"We don't," said Ping.

"*I* want Lady Larchwood to say 'pants'," said Kelpie. "It would be hilarious."

"We don't want her to say 'pants'," Ping repeated. "We want her to say 'pass'. Don't we, Brilliance?"

"Exactly," said Brilliance. "We'll do the pants potion with different ingredients. Lady Larchwood will drink the potion tomorrow morning, and when Dame Fuddle asks her whether she's going to pass or fail St Juniper's, she'll say 'pass'. Easy."

"Brilliant," Sesame breathed.

"So what ingredients shall we use?" asked Kelpie.

Nettle looked around the greenhouse. "Parsley, Applemint, Sorrel and Sage," she suggested. "That spells 'pass'."

The Naughty Fairies scurried to the four corners of the moonlit greenhouse and gathered armfuls of plants. Nettle found a battered walnut shell and a sleepy firefly outside the greenhouse. With a bit of coaxing, the firefly lit up its tail and the potion was soon bubbling.

"It smells delicious," said Tiptoe longingly.

"Much more delicious than 'pants'," said Sesame.

The other Naughty Fairies sniggered.

"What did I say?" asked Sesame, sounding puzzled.

Brilliance peered at Ping's *Mischief*

Monthly in the moonlight. "Stir twice," she read. "Say magic word." She stirred the potion. *"Fala!"* she said, and tapped the cauldron with her wand.

Four bubbles rose to the surface of the potion and popped tunefully. The magic was complete. Now all they had to do was give it to Lady Larchwood.

The Naughty Fairies clustered eagerly around Kelpie at breakfast the following morning.

"Did you do it?" breathed Nettle.

"As planned," said Kelpie, sliding into her seat. "I put a honeycake next to Lady Larchwood's chicory coffee."

Hearing the word 'honeycake', Flea raised his head.

"Flea's drooling again," said Sesame.

Up at the staff table, Lady Larchwood, Lady Rowan and Lady Pollen were all tucking into plates of steaming beech-nut sausages and chatting politely to Dame Fuddle.

"I hope SPARCLE's mysterious

Special Something *is* Sausages," Tiptoe said. "These really are Turnip's best ones ever."

"It's time," said Brilliance importantly. "Do it now, Kelpie."

"Honeycake," said Kelpie, chucking Flea under the chin. "Fetch!"

Flea pelted towards the staff table with his wings in a blur. Straight as an arrow, he flew at the honeycake.

"By Nature!" Lady Larchwood leapt to her feet as Flea raced past her plate and knocked over her chicory coffee.

Kelpie was across the room in a flash. In her best and most apologetic voice, she began mopping up Lady Larchwood's chicory coffee. "I'm so sorry, Lady Larchwood . . . My bumblebee goes a bit crazy sometimes. I should probably exercise him more . . . Here, let me do that."

Kelpie refilled Lady Larchwood's chicory coffee cup – and slipped in a splash of potion.

"Most kind," said Lady Larchwood stiffly, brushing down her gown.

"St Juniper's fairies are extremely polite!" Dame Fuddle jumped in. "Always keen to help! Such a credit to us all! Thank you, Kelpie dear!"

Kelpie went back to her seat and winked at the others. On the floor beneath her, Flea happily crunched through his prize. The Naughty Fairies turned and stared at Lady Larchwood, willing her to take a sip of her coffee.

And at last, Lady Larchwood did.

"Success," said Brilliance. She took a bite out of her clover bun.

"What if someone asks Lady Larchwood a question *before* the question about passing or failing St Juniper's?" asked Sesame suddenly.

Ping frowned.

"Good point," said Nettle.

"Uh oh," said Tiptoe.

"It'll be fine," said Brilliance.

Dame Honey leaned across the staff table and touched the chief SPARCLE inspector on the arm. "Are you enjoying your clover bun, Lady Larchwood?" she asked. "It's one of our cook Turnip's specialities."

The Naughty Fairies held their breath and listened.

"PARP!!!" shouted Lady Larchwood.

6

The Decision

"Excuse me?" said Dame Honey,
looking puzzled.

"PARP!!," shouted Lady Larchwood
again. "PARP! Parp!"

"Lady Larchwood is shouting 'parp',"
said Nettle.

"I *know* she's shouting 'parp',"
Brilliance hissed. "But *why* is she
shouting 'parp'?"

"I think I might have picked the
wrong plants in the greenhouse," said
Sesame sheepishly. "I maybe missed
the sorrel and sage and, um, maybe
picked rue and pennycress instead?"

The others looked at her.

"It was dark," Sesame muttered.

"Parsley, applemint, rue and pennycress," said Ping. "Yup. That spells 'parp'."

"Can everyone stop saying 'parp'?" said Tiptoe. "It's making me gi-hi-higgle . . ."

"My dear Lady Larchwood!" said Dame Fuddle, staring at the SPARCLE inspector. "Is everything all right?"

"Parp!" Lady Larchwood's voice was starting to rise in panic. "Parp! Parp!"

Dame Lacewing swiftly took Lady Larchwood's arm and guided the SPARCLE inspector down from the top table.

"Whatever's the matter, Lupina?" asked Lady Pollen in an anxious voice, hurrying after Lady Larchwood. "Was it something you ate?"

Reluctantly Lady Rowan broke off her conversation with Lord Gallivant and followed Lady Pollen. Round-eyed, the fairies of St Juniper's watched as the three SPARCLE inspectors, Dame Fuddle and Dame Lacewing rushed off between the tables and out through the double doors of the Dining Flowerpot.

Moments later, Dame Lacewing reappeared.

"Brilliance," she said in her most dangerous voice. "Nettle, Sesame, Tiptoe, Kelpie and Ping. Follow me. At *once*."

*

"If I have to look at one more apostrophe, I'll pull its stupid tadpole tail off and throw it back into the Pond," said Kelpie sulkily, looking at the detention paper in front of her.

"Silence," thundered Dame Lacewing.

The Naughty Fairies were sitting in a row in Dame Lacewing's flowerpot classroom. They had written out more than thirty different apostrophe exercises, and there were at least thirty more to go.

"We were only trying to help," Ping muttered.

"Well you haven't." Dame Lacewing slammed her leaf notebook shut. Pipsqueak jumped. "You have just made things worse. The inspectors will now close down St Juniper's, and we shall all be turned out into the Hedge."

The Naughty Fairies were quiet.

"Can't we do anything to make them

change their minds?" Sesame asked in a small voice.

"Believe me," said Dame Lacewing. "You have done more than enough."

The last seed fell from the courtyard dandelion clock and drifted to the ground. A bluebell started ringing furiously.

"Midday," said Ping.

"Decision time," said Tiptoe in a doomed voice.

Flea raised his head, buzzed once and put it down again.

Dame Lacewing stood up. "We had better go into the Assembly Flowerpot," she said. "The inspectors will be waiting for us."

Bright sunlight slanted through the jagged windows of the Assembly Flowerpot, casting interesting shadows on the gathering fairies. The pupils of St Juniper's were impatient to hear the inspectors' verdict. As soon as Lady Larchwood cleared her throat, the whole flowerpot fell silent.

"Good afternoon," said Lady
Larchwood.

"Lady Larchwood's got her voice
back," said Sesame, sounding relieved.

"That's good?" said Kelpie grumpily,
stroking Flea.

"My colleagues and I have spent an
. . . interesting time at St Juniper's
over the past two days," said the white-
haired chief inspector. "And we have

reached a decision regarding the future of this school."

The listening fairies mumbled anxiously at each other for a moment as Lady Larchwood shuffled her papers.

"SPARCLE approves fairy schools on five points," continued Lady Larchwood. "Flying and Fitness. Appropriate Environment. Rigorous Intellectual Development. Tidy Wings and Wands. And our Special Something, which I will come to in a moment. Schools need three passes or more on these points to qualify for the Golden Violet."

The fairies muttered at each other.

Lady Rowan stood up and smoothed down her immaculate jasmine gown. Her hair looked more lustrous than ever. "Flying and Fitness," she said. "Pass."

"I knew that brilliant Sycamore Twist wouldn't be wasted," said Brilliance, punching Nettle triumphantly on the arm.

Lady Pollen patted her rose-pink curls and rustled her papers. "Appropriate Environment," she said.

A piece of flowerpot fell away from the Assembly Flowerpot wall and tinkled on to the ground.

"Fail," said Lady Pollen.

The fairies groaned.

Lady Larchwood took over. "Rigorous Intellectual Development," she said. "Pass."

"I don't believe it," said Sesame in amazement as the fairies cheered.

"Dame Lacewing's Maths lessons must have been very, *very* scary," said Ping, shaking her head.

"Tidy Wings and Wands," continued Lady Larchwood in a chillier voice. "Fail."

"It's all down to the sausages," said Tiptoe, biting her nails.

"And finally, SPARCLE's Special Something," said Lady Larchwood.

The silence in the flowerpot was deafening.

"As you may be aware, this changes with every inspection," said Lady Larchwood. "For St Juniper's, SPARCLE ruled that the Special Something would be Essence of Fairy."

There was a burst of chatter.

"Essence doesn't start with S," said Kelpie in surprise.

"It does," said Sesame. "Sort of."

Lady Larchwood waited for the chatter to die down.

"Essence of Fairy," she said, "is the heart of our nature. It is life. It is zest. It is mischief."

To the Naughty Fairies' astonishment, the chief inspector smiled.

"And on that count," said Lady Larchwood, "St Juniper's has most definitely – passed."

The walls of the Assembly Flowerpot rocked with the cheers which followed Lady Larchwood's announcement. Dame Fuddle began jumping up and down. Dame Honey and Dame Taffeta fell into a hug. Lord Gallivant kissed Lady Rowan on the cheek. Dame

Lacewing put her head in her hands and Pipsqueak tried to lick her ears.

"That was all down to us!" said Brilliance breathlessly, high-fiving the others as hundreds of fairies zoomed up and down and around the flowerpot in triumph. "Brilliant!"

Ping grinned. "Dame Lacewing *totally* owes us one."

"Naughty Fairies FOREVER!" squealed Sesame.

"So the S wasn't sausages after all," said Tiptoe.

"I think you'll get your flutterday feast tonight, Kelpie," laughed Nettle.

"About time too," said Kelpie.

Ping's Wings

It's Bluebell Ball time, but the
Naughty Fairies have more to worry
about than their dresses. Ambrosia
Academy fairy Glitter has challenged
Ping to the Bramble Run: dangerous,
forbidden – and bound to end in
disaster!